James
changes colour

Illustrated by Peter Lawson
Series editor: Teresa Wilson

GULLANE™

Thomas the Tank Engine & Friends

A BRITT ALLCROFT COMPANY PRODUCTION

Based on The Railway Series by The Rev W Awdry

© Gullane (Thomas) LLC 2002

All rights reserved
Published in Great Britain in 2002 by Egmont Books Limited,
239 Kensington High Street, London, W8 6SA
Printed in China
ISBN 0 7498 5487 1

10 9 8 7 6 5 4 3 2 1

Educational consultant: Betty Root, formerly Director of the Reading Centre in the University of Reading.

The Fat Controller liked to see
James puffing along.

His bright red paint shone
in the sun.

But James was cross.

"I'm tired of being a red engine," he said.

The Fat Controller just told him to stop grumbling.

One day, when James was waiting in the station, he saw a big bus.

The bus had flowers all over it.

They were painted in lovely bright colours.

"I want to be painted like that bus," said James. "I want to be painted in bright colours."

"All right, if that's what you want," said The Fat Controller.

The next day, The Fat Controller asked Bridget to paint flowers all over James.

Bridget painted all over the shiny red engine.

Soon James was covered in bright coloured flowers.

James was very pleased with himself.

He wanted all the other engines to see him.

"Thank you, Bridget," he said.

"Anything for you, James," she said.

Lots of children came to look at James.

They all liked his bright colours.

Every time he stopped, bees and butterflies landed on the flowers and tickled him.

Then James began
to grumble again.

"The other engines are all
laughing at my flowers,"
he said.

The Fat Controller told him to stop grumbling.

This only made James cross again.

"I don't like my flowers anymore," he said.

"The other engines are all tired of your grumbling," said The Fat Controller.

He made James sleep outside all night.

It got very dark and James shut his eyes as the rain splashed over him.

"I won't grumble again," he said. But no one heard him.

The next day, the sun shone down on James.

Soon he was warm and dry again.

"Have you noticed anything?" asked
The Fat Controller. "The rain has washed
off all your flowers!"

James laughed and puffed at full speed.

He said, "I really like being red!"

And the other engines liked him red too.